This book is dedicated to Saoirse, Michael and Alfie –
the original Star Girl, Star Boy and Star Pet.
And also to:
Penelope for all she does
Marian for all she's done
And Sam for all he's doing! – J.J.M.

"The little dogs and all –
Tray, Blanch and Sweetheart –
see how they bark at me!" W. Shakespeare

"Yo! Shakespeare!" O. Bickerstaff

Text copyright © J. J. Murhall 1999
Illustrations copyright © Eleanor Taylor 1999

First published in Great Britain in 1999
by Macdonald Young Books
an imprint of Wayland Publishers Ltd
61 Western Road
Hove
East Sussex BN3 1JD

Find Macdonald Young Books on the internet at
http://www.myb.co.uk

Designed and Typeset by McBride Design
Printed and bound by Guernsey Press

British Library Cataloguing in Publication Data available

ISBN: 0 7500 2815 7

J. J. MURHALL
Illustrated by Eleanor Taylor

MACDONALD YOUNG BOOKS

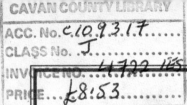

STARRING:-

THE MANIC STREET CREATURES
RAYMOND 'SHAKIN' HARDPAD
QUINCY 'COOL' TRUELOVE
MITCH 'HOUND DOG' MOODY
LITTLE 'FINGERS' TONE

SPECIAL GUEST APPEARANCE:-
OGDEN 'TWINKLETOES' BICKERSTAFF
as 'TITANIA'

CO-STARRING:-
HILARY HARDPAD

FEATURING:-
Fru Fru Lachelle
Colin Curruthers
Ricky Groove
Extras include:- Ponies, cats and dogs.

INSTRUMENTS SUPPLIED BY:-
'Watt. A. Racket' of Bond Street.

Chapter One

"Fancy being a pop star?" asked Little Tone, without moving his lips. The monkey was practising his ventriloquist's skills by holding a Barbie doll in front of his face and waving at the school notice board with one of its arms.

Raymond Hardpad, his terrier friend, gazed up at the board. Pinned in between the third year ballet exam results (Grade 4) and a pony who was selling an exercise bike, was an advertisement.

It read:

Raymond nodded his head enthusiastically.

"You'd be great on guitar, Little Tone. And I'd love to audition for the drums," he declared excitedly.

Little Tone wiggled Barbie's head. "Let's go for it then," he replied, through gritted teeth.

Soon some of the other pupils began to gather around to take a look.

"What's all this about an audition?" snapped Hilary, Raymond's ever-so-scary big sister.

Picking up Ogden the gerbil by the scruff of his neck and dumping him in a nearby plant pot, she pushed her way to the front.

"Oi! Watch my outfit," shouted the Shakespeare-loving gerbil, scrambling out from between the leaves. Ogden brushed down the front of his floaty fairy dress, adjusted his wings and scowled at Hilary. The costume belonged to the wardrobe department and was normally worn in a play called *A Midsummer Night's Dream*. Ogden thought it was one of the finest outfits that he'd borrowed since he'd first arrived at YAPPS a few months ago.

YAPPS was the Young Academy of Performing Pets, the school where pets learnt to be Star Pets. All the animals dreamt of being stars. Ogden wanted to act in Shakespeare's plays.

"Of course it's pointless any of you auditioning," declared Hilary. "Because *I'm* the only potential pop star Star Pet around here."

She scowled at Raymond. "And that includes you, baby brother. Let's face it. The only band you'll ever play with is an elastic one."

Raymond dropped his head and stared sadly at the floor. It was no use arguing with Hilary. You were likely to end up in a whole heap of trouble. However, Little Tone stepped bravely forward. "Stop picking on Raymond. You're nothing but a bully," he declared, clutching Barbie to his chest.

Everyone fell silent. Nobody spoke to Hilary like that! Little Tone gulped but stood his ground as Hilary's top lip quivered and she flashed her sharp white teeth menacingly. Then, raising a bushy eyebrow, she reached out, plucked Barbie from his grasp and yanked her head off. Popping it into her mouth, Hilary gazed disdainfully at the astonished monkey as she chewed on the head like a delicious toffee, finally swallowing it in a single gulp.

11

"You need more practice, Little Tone. I saw your lips move!" declared the dreadful dog, picking bits of soggy plastic out from between her teeth. "Anyway. Now I've eaten most of your act, how about using Raymond? He'd make a *wonderful* dummy."

Just then the bell went for the end of break and Hilary gleefully set off to her next class. It was line dancing this morning and she couldn't wait to tread on some toes.

Chapter Two

Mitch Moody plonked his knee-high pink
cowboy boots up on the table and peered out
from beneath the brim of his enormous Stetson
hat. The bloodhound pup was glum at the best
of times, but this afternoon he was feeling
particularly downhearted. His paws were still
throbbing from the line-dancing class earlier and
now the dog who had trodden on them was
trying her hardest to give him a headache.

Hilary Hardpad sat behind the drum kit playing it like a dog possessed. Every time she whacked the cymbals, the noise vibrated around the room, flew into his ears, hung around for a bit and then finally made itself at home somewhere between his eyes. Mitch grimaced at Quincy Truelove, the saxophonist, who was sitting beside him. Even the normally ice-cool lizard was starting to look a little heated.

Hilary continued to bash away, throwing her head around furiously. Her fur was sticking out in all directions and she looked like a demented troll.

She finally finished by tossing the sticks out of the window and tipping over the entire drum kit with a flourish.

"Well? What do you think? Am I in?" she demanded breathlessly. Mitch and Quincy glanced at each other.

"Well, Hilary. It's like this," replied Quincy, peering at the terrier over the tops of his mirrored sunglasses. Around his neck he wore a lime-green silk scarf and, as lizards go, he was very handsome. "We've already given the job to your brother, Raymond. I know Raymond wants to be a magician, but that dog sure can work some magic on those drums as well. He's one cool dude."

He smiled lazily at her. Quincy Truelove was the only pupil at YAPPS who wasn't afraid of Hilary. He was far too laid-back to be nervous of anyone.

"Raymond's not cool," snapped Hilary. "He couldn't be cool if you shoved his head in a freezer. He's an idiot." Her face brightened as she spotted an electric guitar propped up against the wall. "What about a guitarist? Can't I audition for that?"

Quincy shook his head firmly. "Sorry. We've hired Little Tone. That monkey was probably born with a guitar in his hand. He can even pluck the strings with his teeth."

Hilary stamped her paws crossly.

"How about keyboards then? Our owner, Mrs Bargestorm, used to have a piano."

"Really? And did you play it?" asked Quincy, sounding interested.

"No. I ate it," replied Hilary, looking a little embarrassed.

"What? The whole lot?!" asked Mitch, almost falling off his chair in amazement. Hilary nodded.

"Everything except the keys. I spat them out because they tasted really bitter."

Before Mitch and Quincy could reply, Ogden poked his head around the door.

"Oh no. Not Bickerstaff," muttered Mitch, hiding behind his hat. "That's all we need. A deranged dog and a gerbil who loves Shakespeare joining our band."

Quincy ignored him and beckoned towards Ogden. "Enter dude," he drawled. Ogden scurried in.

"Yo! A gerbil in a dress. Cool," declared Quincy narrowing his eyes and nodding his head sleepily. "This could be a good gimmick for the band."

However, Mitch didn't look too convinced as Ogden clambered up on to the piano stool. "Aren't you a little on the small side to be playing the keyboards?" he asked.

Ogden put his hands on his hips crossly. "Listen. I may be tiny but they don't call me twinkle toes for nothing, you know." And scaling the piano leg like a miniature mountain climber, he pulled himself up on to the keys. Testing one tentatively with his toe, Ogden hoisted up his dress and then proceeded to dance up and down, tinkling out a lovely tune. When he'd finished he sat down breathlessly on the lid. Ogden hadn't 'piano danced' since he was a baby and he'd forgotten how exhausting it could be.

Quincy looked at Mitch and grinned. Mitch shrugged and nodded. He had to admit it. The rodent was good.

"You're in, dude," announced Quincy. "Rehearsals start every Tuesday after school. Madame Swish says she doesn't mind us forming a pop group just as long as it doesn't interfere with our studies."

Ogden was delighted and he slid down the piano leg and hurried off to change his clothes again. He quite fancied being Julius Caesar this evening.

Hilary meanwhile scowled quietly in the corner. Being beaten by her brother was bad enough. But upstaged by a dancing gerbil – the shame of it!

"Couldn't I be your manager then?" she asked desperately, as Mitch and Quincy began to pack away the instruments. "I could bite everyone who didn't buy your records."

"That won't be necessary, my dear girl." A deep
voice boomed out from behind her. Hilary swung
around. Standing in the doorway was an
enormous pig. He was a pot-bellied one to be
precise; very fat and dressed in a smart, navy-blue
double-breasted blazer with a top pocket stuffed
with lollipops. On the top of his head was a single
curl that bounced up and down like a spring as
he walked into the room.

The pig put out a trotter and shook Hilary's paw vigorously.

"The name's Lachelle. Fru Fru Lachelle," he declared, rolling a lollipop around his mouth. "Former YAPPS pupil and, alas, currently out-of-work actor. Quincy and I go back a long way. In fact, I bought him his very first saxophone. It was a plastic one and cost me 99p."

Fru Fru discarded his lollipop stick and immediately unwrapped another one. "He asked me to manage the band, and as I'm currently 'resting', as they say in show business, I accepted. Of course," he added seriously, "I know all about the perils of pop. My brother works in a record shop. It's tough. One week you're the new teen-dream singing sensation and the next..." He waved his lollipop around wildly. "You're on the scrap heap of one-hit wonders."

"Yo! Fru Fru, *I lurve* you, man," exclaimed Quincy hugging his friend. "Come on. Let's go meet the other band members."

And they hurried off leaving Hilary all alone.

"Did you throw these out of the window, young lady?" demanded Madame Swish, the principal, sweeping into the room a moment later, brandishing a pair of drumsticks.

Hilary shook her head. "No, Madame," she lied.

The principal eyed her suspiciously. "Well someone did, because I've just had a complaint from a very angry passer-by. Apparently these drumsticks came hurtling out of an upstairs window earlier and bounced straight off his head. It was a good job he was wearing a hat."

Hilary tried not to giggle as she smiled slyly at Madame Swish. "Perhaps it was Raymond, Madame. Maybe becoming a pop star has gone to his head. He'll be chucking TV sets out of the window and trashing hotel rooms next. I don't know what's come over him lately. He used to be such a nice boy."

Madame Swish put the sticks down on the piano lid and closed the window. "I do hope it won't affect his proper Star Pet training," she sighed, heading towards the door.

"Don't worry Madame," Hilary called out as the principal hurried back to her office. "In the words of a fat pig I just met, I'll make sure Raymond's well and truly plugged in on the perils of pop."

Hilary sniggered as she picked up the sticks and nibbled the ends thoughtfully. Her snivelling little brother was about to become a pop star and Hilary Hardpad, the Queen of meddling mutts, had to act fast.

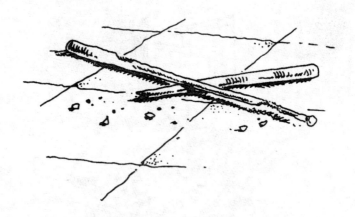

Chapter Three

Raymond's first rehearsal as a *Manic Street Creature* was not going well. His drum kit seemed to have taken on a life of its own. From the very first moment he'd begun to play, the whole thing, including his stool, had started to vibrate.

Raymond was now sitting behind it, shaking like a leaf and bouncing up and down on his seat, trying desperately to stay on. His sticks were nothing but a blur, and his teeth were chattering so much he thought they might shatter.

The others played on, trying to ignore the strange sight behind them. Fru Fru Lachelle had brought along a friend and very important guest.

Ricky Groove, Record Producer of the Moocho Moocho Marvellous Music Recording Company, or Mmmm for short, had come along to listen. This man could turn almost anyone, be it boy, girl or even fish into a pop sensation overnight. However, he'd never seen anything quite like this before. When the song had finished he flicked his ponytail and beamed at his pot-bellied friend.

"This lot are really great," he enthused. "But the dog on the drums... he's out of this world!"

"I've no idea what's wrong with the kit," declared Fru Fru, offering him a lollipop. "But don't worry Ricky. We'll soon get it repaired."

"Don't you fix a thing!" cried Ricky Groove, leaping up from his seat.

"We've got a real pop sensation here," he shouted. "I love the bloodhound in the boots and the gerbil in a dress. I also like the way the monkey sings harmonies without moving his lips and that lizard is really cool. But the best thing about this group is most definitely the little dog and his vibrating drum kit!"

Ricky Groove put an arm around Fru Fru's shoulder. "He's cute, in an ugly, little-dog-lost kind of way. But we need an image for him. What about 'Shakin' Raymond, the Trembling Terrier'? Or how does 'Magic Mutt – He'll Put a Spell On You' sound? Listen, Fru Fru, if we record the song tomorrow we could have a hit on our hands by the end of next week."

He handed Fru Fru his card. It was gold and shaped like a trumpet.

Ricky Groove grinned over at Raymond. "See you tomorrow, Shaky," he said, giving him the thumbs up. The terrier smiled back. Although the drum kit had finally stopped vibrating, Raymond most certainly hadn't.

"See y'-y'-you t'-t'-t'-tomorrow M'-M'-Mr G'-G'-Groove," he stuttered.

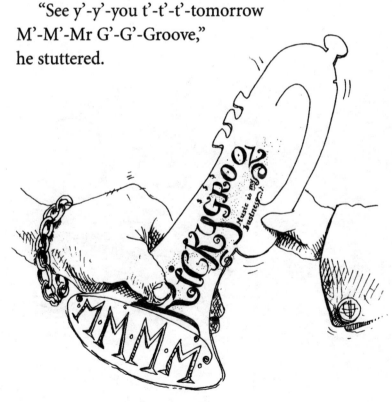

Twenty minutes later, with the tips of his ears still quivering, Raymond and The Creatures were eating their tea in the dining hall along with the other first-years. Everyone wanted to know whether it was true that the soles of Ricky Groove's shoes were made of solid gold and if he really had a diamond embedded in one of his teeth.

Hilary sat alone at the end of the table, scowling into her beans on toast. As Raymond passed his sister to get himself another glass of milk, something in her open school bag caught his eye. Nestling in between Hilary's tap shoes and tights was a book entitled *Electronics for Dogs Made Easy* by B.A. Brightspark.

"Did you tamper with my drum kit, Hilary?" frowned Raymond.

Hilary nodded. "I wired it up during my lunch break. Clever little dog, aren't I? Though it was meant to stop you playing properly, not turn you into some sort of amazing musician. 'Shakin' Raymond!' I've never heard anything so ridiculous," she scoffed.

Raymond sighed. "Can't you just be happy for me, Hilary?"

Hilary shook her head, plunging her fork into her beans on toast. "Never," she snapped. "Now get lost before I take a look at Chapter 5. It's all about how to wire your little brother up and launch him into space."

Raymond hurried away. Hilary probably wasn't joking. She'd have him strapped to a rocket quicker than he could say 'pop star' if he wasn't careful.

Chapter Four

Colin Carruthers, an enormous carthorse and the biggest pupil in the whole school, trotted into the Monday morning maths class, looking very excited indeed. For once he wasn't crying and everyone stared at him in amazement. Colin was always homesick and had shed enough tears to fill a bath since he'd arrived at YAPPS. But now he was grinning from ear to ear.

"Yo, Colin. My main horse. What's happenin', big guy?" Quincy Truelove called out from the back of the class.

"I'll tell you what's happened," replied Colin, breathlessly weaving his way in between the desks. "I was brushing my teeth just now, and listening to the radio, when they played your song, *Mud Puppy Blues*."

"Cool." Quincy polished his sunglasses and grinned at the other band members.

"But better than that," continued Colin eagerly, taking a seat and pulling out his maths book. "It's only gone straight to Number One!"

Mitch sat up in his chair and let out a long, low whistle. "Number One in the whole country. That's amazing."

"Not just in the whole country," added Colin hastily as Mr Willoughby, the maths tutor, entered the room. "It's also topping the charts in every other country in the world! The DJ said that this has never happened before in the history of pop music!"

The group stared in astonishment at each other, except for Ogden – his chair was empty. Mr Willoughby peered over the top of his desk.

"Ogden Bickerstaff, what on earth are you doing down there?" he demanded.

Ogden, who was dressed as a Roman soldier this morning, was now lying flat out on the floor, still clutching his spear. It had all been too much for the tiny gerbil and he'd fainted. He was about to become a piano-dancing superstar. Whatever would his mum say? She would certainly be very proud of her youngest son when she heard the news.

Mr Willoughby frowned as Ogden began to mumble something under his breath. "What's he saying?" asked the teacher, fanning his pupil with a calculator. The whole class stared blankly down at their little classmate and shrugged.

"What a baby! I think he's asking for his mummy," sniggered Hilary.

Colin's eyes began to fill with tears. "I know how he feels," he sniffed, reaching for the tissues. *Again.*

"Wait a minute," declared Little Tone, moving closer. "It sounds like Shakespeare to me."

Suddenly, he leapt back as Ogden sat bolt upright, blinked once and called out, "Mummy, Mummy. Wherefor art thou Mummy?" Then he jumped up, ran up the teacher's trouser leg and began to dance a jig on his desktop. He would have danced until break time if Mr Willoughby hadn't ordered him to sit down and get on with his fractions.

"Even pop stars have to do sums you know," declared the teacher turning to face the blackboard. The whole class groaned. Maths was *so* boring. A potential Star Pet would much rather be tap-dancing than learning their two-times table.

Chapter Five

Mud Puppy Blues was played endlessly on the radio and Raymond's distinctive sound pulsated across the airwaves. It had now become known as 'Dog Drumming' and many other groups were beginning to copy it.

However, the band themselves couldn't leave the school without being mobbed by hoards of screaming fans. Raymond suffered the worst. He had become a pin-up pup for every teen magazine. He'd even had tufts of his fur pulled out when venturing to the shops but, worst of all, someone had broken into his bedroom and stolen his underpants *and* his beloved magician's costume.

Raymond was beginning to have serious doubts about being a pop star. It was all turning out to be extremely dangerous. He certainly hadn't bargained on becoming bald (he'd have to buy a wig at this rate), having his knicker drawer rifled through or being robbed. So Raymond decided that he would pluck up courage and tell everyone how he felt.

At break-time, he found the others flopped out in the common room. It had been a hectic week: filming *Top of the Pets*, playing live on MTV and doing a fashion shoot for *Animal Antics* magazine. All this, and Madame Swish had still insisted that they continue with their studies.

Raymond sat down beside Quincy on the sofa. "I've got an announcement to make," he said.

The others looked up.

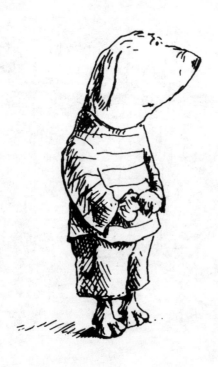

"I'm afraid I'm leaving the group."

Raymond waited for a reaction. Then Quincy smiled, Ogden let out a squeal, Mitch nodded approvingly and Little Tone did a somersault over the back of the sofa.

"We feel the same, Raymond dude," replied Quincy. "We just ain't happy being pop stars. All of us want to be a different sort of Star Pet when we leave YAPPS." Quincy indicated each of the animals in turn.

"Mitch here intends to move to Nashville and become a Country and Western singer. And Ogden? Well, we all know what this little fella wants to be."

Ogden stood up on the arm of the sofa. "I'm going to join the Rodent Shakespeare Company of course, and become a serious actor," he declared, taking a bow.

Everyone smiled as a teddy bear appeared over the top of the sofa and a voice piped up from behind it. "I'm going to be a ventriloquist and Raymond wants to be a magician."

Little Tone's face popped up alongside the bear and he winked at his room-mate.

"And what better place to train than YAPPS?" replied Raymond, looking around him at the vast common room, with its high ornate ceilings and paintings of famous former pupils hanging on the walls. The room was crowded with other students.

Some ponies were chatting and sharing a cola. A couple of cats were showing each other dance steps and a group of dogs were giggling together. Everyone agreed it was certainly a special kind of school and most animals would give anything to have their owners send them there.

They saw Fru Fru Lachelle hurrying towards them, his cheeks bulging with lollipops. The big pig grinned and pointed to his mouth. "I'm celebrating," he announced, though it sounded more like, "Mmmcelerbarratin," as he crunched greedily.

Quincy smiled kindly up at his friend. "I'm afraid *The Creatures* have split up, my lolly-licking friend," he sighed.

Fru Fru stared at Quincy over his swollen
cheeks. "But that's great!" he spluttered. " 'Cause
I've got a job. I'm doing panto this Christmas in
Basingstoke. It's *Puss in Boots* – and guess what?
Old Fru Fru here is playing the Puss! I didn't
much like being a manager anyway. I need the
roar of the crowd and the smell of the greasepaint
too much."

Everyone agreed that Fru Fru was a true Star Pet and that playing a cat when you were actually a pig was a very difficult job indeed.

When he'd gone, Madame Swish came over to tell them that a vanload of Gold Discs had just arrived. "Perhaps you'd like to hang them in the foyer?" she suggested. "As a reminder of your first taste of stardom."

Raymond stared up at her. "Actually, we've agreed to auction them off for the RSPCA."

"What a nice idea," smiled Madame Swish. "Anyway, rehearsals start for the end-of-term production next week so you'll all have a chance to perform again. And Raymond, I thought it might be nice if you warmed up the audience by doing some magic tricks."

Raymond's face dropped. "I can't, Madame. Someone's stolen my magician's outfit. The Great Raymondo can't perform without his cloak and hat."

Madame Swish patted the top of his head. "I've managed to retrieve your costume. A fan swapped it for a packet of coloured pencils and a half-eaten sausage roll. The thief in question was a dog wearing a black plastic coat and a gold-coin collar. But I'm afraid your knickers are long gone. Sold to the highest bidder, no doubt."

Everyone guessed who the thief was, including Madame Swish. "When I catch up with that sister of yours she's in for a nasty shock," she declared crossly. "Because Hilary certainly won't be performing in the show. She'll be working backstage shifting scenery, where she can't get up to any mischief." The Principal glanced quickly around, before hurrying off to check whether Hilary was hiding in the toilets.

In an armchair across the room, Hilary Hardpad buried her nose behind her favourite book. On her lap, there was a packet of coloured pencils and a smattering of pastry crumbs. Biting crossly on a pencil, she scanned the pages for a possible chapter on 'Messing with Magic Tricks'. If she could only wire up her brother's crummy magic set, then his end-of-term act really would go with a bang!

Hilary wasn't beaten yet. Shifting scenery was a mug's game and the all-round bad pet of YAPPS had no intention of ruining her nails. Besides, the end-of-term production was a must for any 'wannabe' Star Pet. Everyone who was anyone would be there and there was no way she was going to miss out. Hilary turned the page, pondering her next move. Then, polishing off the blue pencil stub, she licked her lips and helped herself to a yellow one.

Look out for more Star Pet adventures:

Star Pets on Stage

Welcome to YAPPS (the Young Academy of Performing Pets) where pets learn to be stars! It's a great day for the school when Woodruff the guinea-pig gets a chance to audition for a Hollywood producer. Timid Woodruff has the talent to go all the way to the top. But someone is determined to spoil his big day...

Star Pets on Screen

It's panic stations at YAPPS when Brittany, the air-headed bunny, gets the chance to appear in a TV soap commercial. Brittany thinks that she will become a soap star, but she hasn't bargained for the slippery Hilary Hardpad, a massive shoe sale and two all-action stunt cats...

Star Pets in the Spotlight

The end-of-term show is the chance for the pupils at YAPPS to shine. With tap-dancing horses and a rabbit dressed as a pig, the stage is set for a great show. But with meddling Hilary Hardpad in charge of sound effects, things are sure to go with a bang!

For more information about Mega Stars, write to: *The Sales Department, Macdonald Young Books 61 Western Road, Hove, East Sussex BN3 1JD*